PORTRAITS
OF THE
HEART

GITURA MWAURA

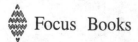

Focus Books

Portraits of the Heart
First published in 2002 by
Focus Publications Ltd
P.O. Box 28176
Nairobi
email: focus@africaonline.co.ke

© Gitura Mwaura, 2001

ISBN 9966-882-65-0

Printed by
English Press
P.O. Box 30127
Nairobi

Poet

You abandon to your self
The bundle that is you
Of romances of the world
And life's endless tragedy
For this is who you are
Who sing portraits of the heart

Poet

CONTENTS

Content

THEURI

Question not the fore-
Ward. Came end
Came new beginning.
The acorn must
Become the oak.
There's nothing to explain.

THE PEOPLE OF NG'ENDA could be seen going about their business with the rustic confidence that comes with nature's goodwill. The sky was blue, with the sun gently streaming down the rolling hills and valleys below, and a gentle breeze was blowing as if to punctuate the general calmness. Coffee in the fields was slowly ripening and the food crops looked healthy after the April rains. Boys and girls could be heard laughing jovially across the fields, their joyous laughs intermingling with the mooing from the cows and the occasional bah from the goats. It was a melodious monotony that conformed well with the prevalent serenity. All was well.

Beneath this façade however, on Gikonyo's compound, all was not well. On it could be seen a house whose walls were plastered white with ochre, and had gleaming iron sheets on the roof. On its left were three grass-thatched granaries two feet above the ground on their stilts. On its right was a grass-thatched hut that, a year ago, had been hurriedly built to house a passing couple and their one child, Theuri. Cows could also be seen grazing beyond the fence and, further beyond, coffee trees. The compound was immaculate; a sign that it was well run.

Gikonyo's wife, Wangeci, a slim, good looking woman of a warm bearing, was seated behind the house sorting out beans. And running around her was young Theuri, yelling excitedly as he chased butterflies. That Theuri could run around with nothing on his mind but butterflies seemed amusing to her.

"Children are happy little things for all they know," Wangeci mused, her calm features breaking into a weak smile. Her fondness for him made her wish she had a child of her own. She would glance at him every now and then to make sure he didn't stray too far or hurt himself.

It was eight years now since she got married to Gikonyo, but it wasn't until after the first year she had finally confirmed that she was indeed barren. Aged thirty now, she led a miserable life of self-pity, her only consolation being The Holy Bible and her sister's children who often came to stay with her, not to mention Theuri.

Gikonyo, on the other hand, had often been pressed by his peers to marry a second wife. But being a staunch Christian he would hear nothing of that, let alone think of it. "It is a sin to have two wives," he always stressed. "Even Abraham had to bear with Sarah's barrenness before she bore him Isaac", he added, and prayed every day. So both he and Wangeci had lived with a shared belief that they would one day get a child. Still, Wangeci could not help envying Theuri's mother who lived in the hut next to her house.

It was almost a year ago, she remembered, when Gikonyo arrived home one late evening with a weary couple and their one child. He had introduced them as Mutahi and his obviously pregnant wife, Njeri—Wangeci had especially noted the pregnancy. But it wasn't until after they were fed and settled that their ordeal had been unfolded to her.

Mutahi and his family had been squatters in Mang'u at a farm belonging to a colonial settler named George Smith, who was famed for his

9

excellent relations with the Africans. Mutahi had been born, bred and had married there. But due to his close associations with the white man, to the extent he had access to the white man's imposing mansion at any time of day or night, he had been branded an informer; a terrible accusation to have been made on anyone. He and his family had however lived happily in a provided small plot, until that night of the day before they arrived with Gikonyo. That night, Mau Mau freedom fighters had struck, killing the white man and his family, including his servants and some squatters. Mutahi's hut being at a distance from the rest had saved his life. In the nick of time, he had fled with his small family and hidden in the coffee plantation.

After all was quiet he had stolen from their hiding place and had learnt of the killings, which included his wife's entire family—also reputed to be of informers. Mutahi had no other family, himself having been born of a single mother who had long died with no other known relatives except Mutahi.

Thus with no family left in their lives they had no life there, not to mention they could not be safe there even for one more day. So going to Nairobi to find a job had seemed the only way out to Mutahi. And early the next morning, after making burial arrangements for his wife's unfortunate family, they were on their way, keeping mainly to the coffee plantations.

That was when they were to meet with Gikonyo on his way home from some place, Wangeci could not remember exactly where.

Having walked all day, Gikonyo could see that they were tired and probably hungry when he looked at their son. So, he had struck a conversation with Mutahi, from whom, though wary at first, the story had poured out.

Gikonyo, moved by their tragedy, had sympathetically welcomed them to his home and later that night had convinced them to stay, at least on account of Njeri's pregnancy and their young son, Theuri. It would do no harm to stick with them a few months until after Njeri had given birth, Gikonyo had argued. And Mutahi, though not one to impose himself or his own on anybody, had nevertheless agreed. The next day a hut was built and they had settled down to their new and temporary life in Ng'enda.

In the ensuing two months, things went on well. Mutahi and Njeri were helping where they could and the two couples grew quite close to each other. This was until one morning when Mutahi had taken a walk and never returned.

With the help of neighbours they had tried to look for him, or his body, but in vain. After a few days they had given up, assuming him a victim of Mau Mau's unrelenting vengeance on informers.

It was supposed he had gotten wind of the presence of freedom fighters nearby, or perhaps he feared that the Mau Mau's broad intelligence network would most certainly catch up with him. Most speculated that he had decided to divert attention from his family and host by disappearing. Whatever it was, it would never be known.

It was incredible though that Mutahi should suddenly disappear, and Njeri not knowing what to do couldn't help feeling desolate despite Wangeci's consolations. Days crawled and about two months later their second son, Muya, was born.

Seven months had gone by since and looking at Theuri, Wangeci wondered what would become of this three-year-old who seemed brighter than his age. She also failed to understand why tragedy after tragedy kept hitting this family.

That previous Wednesday afternoon, a week to the day, while seated at the front of the house with Njeri chatting and weaving baskets, Njeri had suddenly informed her that she was not feeling well and was going in to relax. When evening came she was vomiting, with the situation getting worse during the night. So the next morning Wangeci, accompanied by Gikonyo, had taken her to the hospital at the Catholic Mission seven miles away. She was admitted with Muya and had so far not improved. Yesterday when Wangeci had been to see her she looked thin and very weak. Wangeci had thus stayed with her trying to make her eat but she wouldn't. So, returning home discouraged and tearful, Wangeci felt the more depressed because the doctor, who was Father Giusseppe of the Catholic Mission, would not release the seven-month-old Muya saying he had a certain infection, "though it was not serious," even though his mother was producing little milk, if any at all.

"Look what I've caught," said Theuri excitedly, suddenly cutting her reverie. So engrossed was she in the unhappy reminiscence that Wangeci didn't hear him approach.

"Yes? What have you caught?" she inquired managing a smile.

Theuri opened a small tightly clenched fist to reveal a crushed butterfly.

"It is beautiful, isn't it?" And Theuri nodded happily as Wangeci continued, "but you should never hold them that tight again, you could easily kill them." She advised in a motherly tone.

"But it is not dead. Look! It's breathing," replied Theuri defensively as the breeze shook the dead butterfly.

"I can see," said Wangeci returning to sort out the beans. "Where did you catch it?"

"Over there," Theuri pointed, then, sensing what was on Wangeci's mind, he suddenly asked, "Is mother coming today?"

"No, the doctor said she will have to stay a little longer because she has not recovered yet."

"Will you take me with you tomorrow?"

"Yes, I will," she promised.

"I hope father will be there," he said as he hurried off to chase more butterflies. His father was still fresh in his memory...

The tall man approached the gate. He had the physique of an accomplished athlete with a humble, docile air about him. Theuri looked up as Gikonyo walked the path to the house. Having tired of running around he had settled down to build himself a hut. His face brightened as he excitedly waved at Gikonyo who waved back and forced a smile that didn't quite come off as he got into the house. Theuri's young memory could not recall him look like that before, so he felt rather than thought Gikonyo was not happy. But that did not trouble him, his immediate problem was his unfinished hut.

Finally bored with his own company, Theuri walked to the house and stood on the earthen floor feeling the changed atmosphere. And as if to locate the reason for the change, his eyes swept the scantily furnished living room before settling on Gikonyo and Wangeci by the kitchen door.

Wangeci immediately started weeping on seeing him while Gikonyo wondered how to break the news to this wide eyed infant.

"Why is mother crying?" Theuri asked with concern, surprising even himself for he had never referred to Wangeci like that before. Yet it somehow seemed right.

"Come over here," responded Gikonyo beckoning him to sit on his lap. "You see," he started to say thinking of how to phrase the words, "She is crying because your mother won't be coming home."

Theuri was baffled. "Why?" he asked.

"She died this morning," Gikonyo answered quietly with his voice barely audible, hoping that he would understand.

Theuri looked at him with disbelief. His mother dead? How could she die.

He then looked at Wangeci and remembered the butterfly he had killed in the morning, then everything came to him and he started to cry.

SONJA

NEARLY TWO YEARS before we see Sonja writing a letter she intended Charlie should not forget for as long as he had memory, something that, for lack of a better word, can only be accorded to serendipity, happened. It was to have a deep bearing on the letter we are about to witness being written. So it might be well if we first recalled that little incident.

It happened on the day Sonja moved into her furnished apartment. It was situated on the fourth and last floor of a residential block in a quiet, tree-lined suburb area like one finds in many cities. For all practical purposes, it promised to afford her domestic ease and peace of mind, and also suit her working atmosphere perfectly.

But the apartment featured a minor flaw—an in-built wooden bureau at her favoured working spot by the bay window. It was obvious that the bureau had been converted by some not-so-careful tenant or other from what had initially been a sideboard of some kind. In effect, therefore, it was the only piece of furniture that did not bear the uniformity nor the taste exhibited in all the others. For this reason Sonja had deemed it appropriate to have it replaced to restore the apartment's full glory, and had gone on to contract a carpenter to do the work.

As it happened the carpenter arrived on the day Sonja moved into her apartment. As she watched him work, while good humouredly delving in small talk with the agreeable carpenter, Sonja felt inclined to offer her hand to help in the dismantling, seeing the carpenter was having a little trouble. Oblivious to the carpenter, however, and as all discoveries are stumbled upon, it was in the course of this helping that Sonja took sight of a clipped sheaf of papers that had been lodged between the back of the bureau and the wall.

Suffice it to say that Sonja forgot all about the carpenter, who took little notice of this development. She took in the typed contents on each of the five leaves of paper with increasing trepidation for as she read through them, it was as if she was reliving her life with and after Charlie. It was as if their author, who for some reason had signed an unsteady single letter initial, "W", in faded blue ink at the bottom of each of the five papers, had been the one who had lived her life.

We must leave it to Sonja to reveal the contents of her discovery. But how had the poems been forgotten where she discovered them? For how long had they been there? What kind of man was their author, this "W"?

These questions were imponderable, but Sonja felt that she could at least glean part of the answer from what she had read. Still, it seemed that the unsteady initial, "W", which was identical on all the papers, could be more revealing. It seemed suggestive that the life of the hand that had so unsteadily signed it had started at a summit, not unlike the high point of the first stroke in the "W", sliding painfully down to a dark time before rising painfully again to a summit of joy that was immediately followed by another painful drop, before triumphantly rising to the top of the final summit to complete the "W".

If Sonja understood herself, she felt that she knew this man as one can ever know a person. She perceived a young man, who just like herself, for she was twenty three years old, was in his early to mid twenties. And in her certainty, a man of a somewhat melancholic disposition, blue, as it were, just like the ink he had used to sign his initial.

Why this should seem so is difficult to determine. Perhaps she saw in the poems a consolation in her decided solitude at her new abode, or even an accomplice in the poet who it seemed had found his self in this very apartment. Or perhaps it was that her's was a forlorn soul seeking refuge in the happy imagined. Whatever it might be, we can only speculate. But in those few moments it took her to read and ponder over the contents of her discovery, their author became as vivid as flesh and blood. He became the man she henceforth came to know by the name, Blue Dubliew (W).

As a consequence to this, perhaps to keep it as a constant reminder of the man who once used it, Sonja suddenly changed her mind about the bureau. It came to her that in trying to make the apartment flawless, she was denying it the very quality that had drawn her to it; the obnoxious bureau that in its contrasting essence made her appreciate the good taste, the beauty even, in all the other fixtures.

Thus spying on the visible change that had suddenly occurred in his brief employer, as evidenced by her shaking hands and the yellowed sheaf of papers which rustled so noisily, the carpenter could not hide his consternation that out of nowhere, Sonja should suddenly change her mind and ask him to reassemble the bureau that now lay in a pathetic heap on the carpeted floor. Sonja, who did not trust herself to explain this change of mind, did not bother to try. But she was going to pay for the trouble, which was as good a reason as any for the bewildered carpenter.

Now, so that we may proceed to the writing of the letter we deferred, it should be noted in passing that what happened in the ensuing one year and nine months offers us no interesting insights, nor is it relevant to the matter at hand, which brings us to this day where we see Sonja in the quiet confines of her apartment seated at the now reassembled bureau by the bay window.

Before her stood a computer, a confirmation of her residency in the so called cyberspace. This she used to network with her advertising clients and, indeed, the world. She could have used the computer to write the letter and e-mail it, but had decided not. This was because other than making the letter memorable, she also wanted it to have that personal feel, which meant writing it by hand. Thus she had pushed the computer key panel to the side to accommodate a writing pad.

To her right lay Charlie's typed note. She had received it that morning and, unsurprisingly, by the look of the envelope that contained it, it had changed hands severally to reach her because of her having to change her address when she moved into the apartment. The note simply read:

Dear Sonia,

How are you doing, darling? It's been a long time. I wish to see you again. Could you allow me the pleasure of your beautiful company?

I lack for words, and all I can say until that happy moment is for you to give us another chance. I want you back.

Could you please contact me?

Love,
Charles Mogera.

This note, which seemed to Sonja a little too brash and assuming, did not reveal a Charlie different than she had known. She tried to imagine how he would look like now but her mind would not accommodate. It seemed embroiled in feelings that translated themselves into suggestive imagery, among which stood out a loom, so that there was no coherence in her thoughts whatsoever. She had been in this state of mind all this while she had been seated at the bureau trying to write a reply that would not come into formulation. Hers was not unlike a mind engaged in an elusive task that wandered in all sorts of seemingly irrelevant imaginations other than concentrate on the task it was employed. In her case, the imaginations included the seemingly indissoluble loom.

This image was worth a little reflection, for in their dance, the warp and the woof in the loom might have been her and Charlie back in time. Yet she watched uncomprehendingly in her mind's eye as the threads weaved a fabric which, after having come to full completion, resplendent in flowery decorations, parted with the loom taking a glorious life all its own. This might have been love. For is it not so with love, in its warp and woof, to uplift the lovers' hearts into a glorious world all their own? But at what point in time does this fabric—this love, begin to totter and then fade? Of this the jilted lover might enlighten us, but we must get on with Sonja.

Unable to coax her unyielding mind to suggest a fitting reply to Charlie's note, Sonja gazed through the bay window at the blue sky and hazy mid-morning horizon as if her troubles might find their solution there. Then she picked the note to read it again. It was then she discovered the misspelling in her name.

The misspelling was with the barely noticeable letter 'i' instead of 'j' in the "Dear Sonia" on the note. It proved to be the same when she checked the address on the envelope to confirm whether it had been a mere typographical error.

This was to sober her immediately. And in her now released mind, like a balloon suddenly pricked into letting out all the built up pressure inside it in a burst, she thought to herself with vicious resentment, "Why, he can't even spell my name properly!"

It mattered little to her that even with the misspelling, her name — son-yah — still pronounced somewhat the same with the letter 'I'. If the truth be told, Sonja had a fetish with letters which, taking the special characteristics that define each, could be inferred to symbolize more all by itself than it normally would in its mere participation towards the forming of a word. It was one of those idiosyncrasies one might find in the habit of some of those people who work with symbols. That is why, for example, Blue Dubliew in his unsteady initial that was to earn him his name with Sonja, seemed to make so much sense. And to demonstrate her incurable fetish with letters to express herself, a rather predictable thought passed through her mind.

"For my doubts about what would come of his wanting me back," Sonja thought to herself, "he has dotted the 'i'."

On this thought, Sonja picked up a biro to begin her reply.

Dear Charlie,

I've just received your letter(!) to which I owe gratitude for the dilemma I now find myself in wondering whether to feel relieved or flattered that you want me back after all this time.

The letter(!) says it all and if, as it suggests, you are the same man I knew, I can divine your state of mind and shan't insult its earnesty by inquiring after how you are doing. (Ha. Ha. I can imagine you saying to yourself now as you read this, "Just like her to rub it in." Not to worry.)

But let me not mislead you into thinking this a laughing matter, for though you have ever been on my mind, I...

Sonja paused abruptly in her writing unsure of how to proceed, the reason being none other than Blue Dubliew. Until that moment, because he formed the core of all she wanted Charlie to know, she had taken it for granted that she would know how to put it. Indeed, Blue Dubliew was so real to her that before she stopped writing she wanted to say, "met another man," to complete the sentence. But how to put the unlikely details behind her relationship with Blue Dubliew without provoking Charlie's mirth, in whose guffaws of laughter she would be dismissed as insane?

Sonja put down the biro and let her now frantic mind do its work to get her out of this little dilemma. She briefly gazed at the computer screen and, as usual, thought nothing of the grotesquely disfigured reflection of her beautiful self that stared back at her. But in a flash she knew how the letter must be written. The one she had started to write, she admitted to herself, was a little contrived— insincere, just like an advertising copy for one of her clients. Now she would simply let herself go, fetish and all. And in her zeal would faithfully let her man, Blue Dubliew, speak for himself word for word in the letter. The result would bear the semblance of a pastiche, but hers was hardly a literary intention.

The unfinished letter Sonja tore from the pad, crumpled it and unceremoniously tossed it into the waste-paper basket. Then, with a rapid cursive hand, she began to write the startling missive.

Dear Charlie,

Thanks for your letter. It was very nice of you to remember me after such a long time. However, I wish to begin by saying that a lot of water has passed under the bridge and, if I may, I wish to immediately start by showing you how much, gallon by gallon:

> The sun shone in solitude
> After the storm, and I
> Was cast in a grey cloud.
>
> What had happened between us
> (As all in love wonder how)
> I can only try but briefly paint,
>
> For the rainbow had arched its way
> Vivid for all to see
> The path of our smitten hearts.

Our journey, though no less
Colourful, was mostly smooth
But parochially wheedling

That, unable to turn,
I kept wiping my brow
As the sun emerged its untainted light

When this it finally dawned,
That this thing love, like the rainbow,
Is just a mist with a myth.

You need no reminding, Charlie, but that's our story to a 't', after which I walked away disillusioned and lovelorn. And now you say you want me back. Why now? Where were you when I needed you, even after we parted? Do you know that I was ready "to give us another chance," as you put it?

I tried looking for you, but you moved from the house I knew. You changed jobs; you even changed towns. How I searched for you, Charlie. How I searched. You've never known anything like it. The loneliness; the yearning for you. The yearning. Then the sense of betrayal, the pain, the hollowness inside, the self hate, the despair. It

was terrible, Charlie, but you don't know how
terrible.

2359HRS 59"

Other than overstay
Like stale wine odour lingers
After the wineskin is done

I'll fly away
Breath unbound
In search of peace

For such it might be
We are born a new
Of our amber sound-crystals
Which, like thought,
Are ever in latent embers-

A warmth thus welcome
In the cold fury of death

I was that far from the zero hour; a heart-beat
away. Yes, I had perceived myself a zero without
you. But on a little thought I hesitated from the
precipice on which I hung. A thought that, if I
was your finished wine, you were mine lost. That,

even so, like the letter 'O' curves back on itself
independent in its regular completeness, I could
be my own wine. I became my own wine.

And now you say you want me back. To what?
Have you forgotten your incessant threats before
we parted?

> Reality is unrelenting
> And selfish—too damned selfish:
> Is it
>> What you meant?
>> What you swore
>> Wanting in me?

> But that I'm singularly secular,
> Is it
>> What you meant?
>> What you swore
>> Wanting in me?

> To seek some almighty
> To strew them wide
> Then I sigh it in?

> No, reality's vanity is nude,
> As nude as coming.

Now, lest you imagine I've confused my G's and Q's, the joke's on me. It is all in humouring myself both as a woman and as a victim. It is cathartic. And if you think I've changed, Charlie—Yes, I have changed.

> Is one a misogynist
> Who detests the woman
> Who at times forgets not
> To be a woman?
>
> Her honesty is engaging, admittedly,
> But I imagine there are truer ways
> To assuage an indifferent heart
> Than strut the stage a nude shadow
> When one can strip at Freedom Corner
> And still hold the beauty
> Of all the flowers in the world.

I am sure you catch my drift, Charlie, and I need not say more. But the 'i' must be dotted:

THE SECRET I WON'T TELL

> I want to be your friend, lady,
> But won't even admit it to tell
> For a tug in my breast
> I thought vanished with a previous other,

Which is another story, but one
I would like to re-write without
Provoking the genie in love.
Of it I disavowed the flesh
Obliterating two other dimensions, time
And space, and was purged by the fourth
When I explored the depths in me
To discover there are more miles within
Than the future can hold —
The moral of which I am still learning
In me, in you, I ever am. Ever.

Yet to oblige a fifth, of magnitude,
I doubt whether you should understand
The hedge between us is all I need;
The secret I won't tell:
I want to be your friend, lady.

*So, Charlie—there! I've said it; I drew the 'X'.
And all, I must confess, in a man I've just shared
with you in those verses. I call him Blue Dubliew.
It may come as a surprise to you to know that I
have never, nor likely ever to set my eyes on him.
But however it may sound, in his decided absence,
he is the one for me. Don't ask me to explain for
I don't understand it either,*

All I know is that
He has lived my woe
And his thread rings
Inextricably with mine
Like the sound of "K"
In the word "croon"—
Never there, but there
Crooning, always—bye
Charlie.

Yours ever,
Sonja Nanjeri.

The flourish with which Sonja signed her name on the letter left little doubt as to her conviction in what she had written. But a while later, we are told, as she searched her drawers for an envelope in which to mail her letter, a certain want suddenly came over her entire being.

We are assured that it would be futile to try and trace the flurry of disjointed thoughts that this derived. But like the bridge in the letter 'H', as no doubt Sonja might have remarked, she and Charlie and the memories between them, good and bad, that ever impinge on people who at one time it occasions to live through a situation of deep

33

intimacy together, they were indelible in each other and nothing could change that.

It is not for us to moralize, but it was that like the bureau she had to change her mind over, in her realization that perhaps it requires a flaw to appreciate beauty, so can it be said that it also suddenly came to her that perhaps it requires a lie to discover a truth — the truth of her self denial in Blue Dubliew who was at best a phantasm, and that of Charlie's genuine if imperfect call for love in his note to her.

Sonja, we are told, had then looked at the letter she had written, read through it once, then tore it to smithereens and reached for the phone.

34

MZEE KIRUI AND HIS RADIO

THIS EVENING, like most others, Mzee Kirui sat in his favourite chair in his comfortably furnished sitting room. Before him burned an electric heater to wade away the creeping cold. And having just fortified himself with his usual vegetarian supper, he was about to give himself to his more absorbing pursuit with his old radio, which culminated in its tuning.

As he readied himself to rouse the old radio from its silence, an owl hooted somewhere. He instinctively looked through a crack in the window curtain from where he sat, as if to locate the owl's haunting voice, and made out that the darkness outside was just beginning to reach its height. And likening it to the Kapsabet society around him where he lived in his wooded farm, the darkness seemed indifferent but rather genial in its necessity, though it somehow accentuated his sense of loneliness. But how it is that old age dwells in the sidelines of a world continually infused with new blood, new values, and the falling one after another of his peers was something he had long learned to live with. And in acknowledging the necessity of growth's unhindered march for the better, he had obliged that the new must outdo the old to a quiet if respectful oblivion.

At ninety six, however, widowed for three years, and unblessed with progeny, it might have been that Mzee Kirui paid the cruel price that was the privations of a lonely existence. But the wily nonagenarian could not claim to be lamentably stricken by the severity of his condition; the gratitude of which he owed his old radio which, like an accomplice in a world of continual innovation, had proved a valuable companion in the otherwise forbidding twilight of his long life.

That old radio, like the withered countenance of its owner, was hardly much to look at, but of dependability it valiantly bore its mettle. It had been in Mzee Kirui's ownership for more years than he cared to remember, though he was apt to mention that he had literally bought it for the proverbial song from a departing Baptist missionary he had befriended in his youth.

The radio, whose brand name had long rubbed off, featured an aged mahogany case out of which was carved a grill for a speaker which was hidden behind a thick browned fabric that at one time glittered with a patterned golden thread. And like the gnarled fingers of their handler, just below the yellowed plastic window that indicated the numbered frequencies, stood out the tuning dial, the band selection and volume buttons, all of which were made of a certain hard black plastic that was crowned with aluminium tips whose golden gild was wearing off. But it also featured a broken bit of a telescopic antennae which Mzee Kirui, with the radio on his lap, was improvisingly extending by attaching a straightened coat-hanger wire for better reception before he turned it on.

The tender manner in which he attended to the old radio on his lap betrayed his dedication to it. It was not without a certain reverence, as if to a peer in whose righteous worthiness he seemed to say, "It is for your courage to remain who you essentially are and your goodwill towards me that I kindly reciprocate." However, this was not what was going through Mzee Kirui's mind, if any thought at all, for the matter at hand which was to restore the radio's voice required a little concentration.

So having fixed the improvised aerial, he turned on the radio but no sound came forth. He knew that it was not the batteries, which he had replaced with new ones only the day before.

"Those cockroaches again," he muttered to himself, then tapped the radio gently and it started to cackle then splattered and whistled, then went silent again. He turned it off then on again, all in one motion, but still no sound came on.

This was normal with the radio, and as Mzee Kirui often explained it to curious visitors, "The cockroaches in it, like the problems of life which no soul is exempt, come from wherever they come from and no matter how you try to eradicate them they always find their way back. The counsel is patience and delicate nursing and the radio will certainly show some cheer."

So Mzee Kirui tapped the radio gently again and this time it crackled once and a steady hissing, or more precisely, a shh-like kind of sound came on.

"There now — hold it there," he urged the radio with a coaxing whisper, betraying a habit that had become normal to him.

But if the cockroaches constituted a problem, they were not the only ones in the radio's experience. An intrinsic problem that came with age and continued use was the band button which needed delicate manipulation before the desired band could hold. Now that the steady hissing sound was on, Mzee Kirui turned this button from 'Medium Wave', the band on which the radio was earlier receiving the national station, Voice of Kenya, trying to hold 'Short Wave band' in order to tune in BBC World Service, his station of choice come evening.

"Just a matter of time now," he spoke to the radio, "and we'll tune us there".

For some time he fumbled with the band button, now turning it, now twisting the tuning dial to gauge his success, but there was no change in the steady hissing sound.

Mzee Kirui understood his radio, and true friendship, as he always made it known, belies its bearer's defects. If the radio exhibited these frailties, it needed him to work. Likewise, he needed it for all it afforded him on such lonely evenings as this. Yet perhaps the radio could be repaired, but there were no existing spare parts anywhere, this type of radio for decades now having been phased out of production.

To those who suggested he buy a digital radio to keep up with the times, just like he and his late wife had with household appliances such as the microwave oven which was much easier to use with their advancing age, Mzee Kirui would rhetorically reply in unremitting solidarity with his outmoded radio, "I am a nonagenarian now, but what could possibly be done about it?" adding, "Whoever heard of a fellow who would take his comforting though imperfect friend for garbage. We just have to bear with each other's deficiencies." This allowed for few arguments, and thus it was that the radio, as exemplified by his tender ministrations to resuscitate its voice, was bonded to him; loving it, as it were, for its faults. Therefore, how long it took to bring it around to speaking terms, so to speak, was besides the point to the nonagenarian.

But suddenly, as he unabashedly continued his ministrations, the radio came alive. On it was a story he could not at first comprehend having caught it in the middle. The male voice on the radio was narrating: *"(Cackle)—the typewriter that had been used to write those lines lacked the letter 'm' and had a crooked 'p'. And their author, faced with the imminent jilt, itched to write something to woo back his lover..."*

Sighing his doubts audibly, Mzee Kirui strained for a moment trying to tell by the accent whether this was the station he sought. "There's a certain guttural ring to it," he explained to the inanimate radio, "It can't be BBC." But before he could touch the tuning dial something urged him to keep listening.

"...Not knowing what to write, while acknowledging that he necessarily needed a replacement for the typewriter because of its defects, an idea had suddenly struck hi—(cackle). Just to humour himself, as he thought of what to

40

*say to his lover, he decided to give the typewriter
a chance in mitigation before he consigned it to
the garbage heap..."*

Mzee Kirui was not sure he quite followed the
drift but determined himself to listen on. He
adjusted a slight shift in the frequency to remove
static and raised the volume a bit.

*"...These were the lines he wrote in defence of
the defective typewriter with a missing 'm' while
using it, in a streak of irony, to do the job. This
made him keep it as a momento after acquiring a
word-processor, but also turned a jilt into a jest
that smiled his lover into reconsideration:*

> That ..y type has a dull 'p'
> And the '..' is fallen,
> Allow, this once, a chance
> In ..itigation:
>
> Before you hitch an u..brella,
> Is it that yesterday's cloud
> Doesn't really set with yesterday's sun?
>
> What about the ..orrow?
> For all it ..ay be,
> Is it not always a ..ixed blessing
> That, it too, ..ight venture its cloud?

41

Please, not to answer,
For this is not a question,
It is that we care;

That, in life's disquietudes,
We love not perfect
But because i..perfect."

After the last line there followed a bridging tune that signified either the end of the program or that it would be continued. But Mzee Kirui was no longer listening as he sat turning those dramatised lines over in his head.

He chuckled suddenly as a thought crossed his mind, then he remarked, "What a coincidence. I am the last person to doubt your sense of humour, but if I didn't know better I'd swear you were the one who urged me to listen on." He was speaking to the radio, but he continued, "Anyway, I'd never discard you, as if I ought to remind you that. Now let's see what we have in BBC." And he twisted the tuning dial to which the radio responded gugglingly like an amused child:

"...Al mudzi zook-(Whistle)-(some oriental music)-espera-(cackle)-is is BBC World Service. In a moment we will bring you a summary of the world news followed by (cackle)-hall, a classical music programme in which we shall feature works by Mozart among others..."

Mzee Kirui moved the radio from his lap and carefully placed it on the stool beside him. Then he sank into his chair contented that the old radio was now in its element. He gloated to himself that after a glimpse of what was in the news summary he would get their full treatment in the 'Newshour'. But being a lover of music, 'from the African drum to the symphony orchestra,' as he was apt to put it, his evening was only beginning towards its customary happy conclusion.

The radio was clear and smooth except for what could be described as excited but unobtrusive bird-like chirps in the background. He thought of these chirpy sounds, forgetting about the news summary, and it occurred to him that if he had anything in common with the flighty creatures, it was that each according to his endowment flew his fancy whither he willed. They, the birds, the clear unencumbered skies. He, the world the radio opened up for him.

But even as this passed through his mind, Mzee Kirui thought that he felt a little stiff and chilly despite the heater. The news was now over and a solemn strain of one of Mozart's piano concertos was going on in the radio. The nonagenarian decided it would be best if he regaled himself with the music in bed, which would most certainly be more comfortable.

With the slow deliberate movements of the

aged, now more pronounced due to the cold that seemed to have invaded his body, he picked up the radio as he rose from the chair. He entered the bedroom, turned on the light and placed the radio on the bedside table. Then he transferred the heater to the bedroom turning off the sitting room light as he did so. He removed his warm cotton pyjamas from the wardrobe and changed into them. After this he entered the bathroom to relieve himself. And as he gave in to a passing shudder, it seemed peculiar that his normally warm pyjamas were failing him, for the cold that had driven him out of the sitting room seemed to be seeping right through to his brittle bones.

He noted that there was an aria going on now on the radio and he tried to remember whose the sad trilling tenor was. It was Luciano Pavarotti's, he decided. Turning off the light, Mzee Kirui got into bed and pulled the thick woollen blanket over himself. The music wafted softly to him. He remembered his wife and the thought of her warmth outside and inside this very bed when once she graced it made him feel a little better.

GRANDMOTHER MUNIRA'S GOAT

IT COULDN'T HAVE COME to that had Grandmother Munira remembered to tie it. You see, it was one of those spirited goats that know no better than to gleefully scamper from one carefully tended garden to another as suited its fancy.

It needs no saying, but such animals could only mean trouble. And when trouble came, it came in the name of Kamau son of Ngariama. To those who knew this young man in the village, and that meant everyone, he was like a curse upon the people who could often be heard agree among themselves, "A good man, Ngariama was. But that son of his - ah!"

A suitable adjective to describe this young man always lacked but the sentiment was never lost.

There was some reason to this. For instance, shortly after his father's death, a troubling thing happened. Now, as you well know, rare are the secrets in the village. So for a long time it had been common knowledge that Kamau was courting a reluctant but beautiful daughter of Kaguta. Trouble was that this girl of his passion was also in someone else's eye—a more agreeable young man from across the ridges to the north. And as time progressed it soon became clear who the girl had decided to marry. A fact which Kaguta, in defence of his daughter, made explicitly clear to Kamau.

But Kamau was another one. After this caution by Kaguta, he could be seen accosting the bride-to-be on her way to the river, trying to make her change her mind. But it was to no avail, which was not surprising. Yet if she had rejected him, it was a rejection that was to earn her and her family unmentionable insults and threats from Kamau.

Then the wedding day came. And that night, after the bride had left her father's home, Kaguta's granary, which had been stocked with that season's ample harvests, had been razed to the ground in a mysterious fire.

Was it an act of arson? Nobody could tell. It might have been sparks blown in the evening breeze, from the ebbing fires that had prepared the excellent wedding feast. Yet again, they might have been not. Nobody saw him, but in most people's minds it was obvious who had done it.

But it was also common knowledge that Kamau had another passion—sweet potatoes. So, as I was saying, Grandmother Munira's goat. It was not clear what happened, but Wandua had seen it larking near Kamau's sweet potato garden. The goat was unmistakable, for its coat of fur, which was otherwise white, had black streaks that ran along both lengths of its body, to join at its black stub of a tail.

Now, on his way back, Wandua had noticed that Kamau's healthy sweet potato vines had been extensively damaged throughout the garden. But there was no sign of the goat. Wandua had felt sorry for Kamau, but not without a tinge of amusement. For in his peculiar ways, Kamau was known to live on sweet potatoes almost exclusively. This was mid-day, and thinking no more of it, Wandua had hastened on home to tend to his own troubles, his wife having recently deserted him. But he was quick to remember that Kamau had long sworn that whichever goat made the mistake of treading upon his garden, "that would be the day!" Kamau had never elaborated.

So the day progressed, and come evening Grandmother Munira was confident that her goat, which she had named Mareka, would make its way home from its excursions. She waited. The goat never showed up. Likewise the following day she waited, still evening came and the goat was nowhere to be seen. Alarmed finally, on the third day she started early in the morning in search of Mareka, her goat.

Now, Grandmother Munira was well liked and respected, and in her advanced age it seemed everyone's duty to look out for her well-being. So those she met in her search joined in and together they scoured in vain every likely place in the village. In her distress, sympathy abounded and soon it was on everyone's lips that Mareka was missing.

Meanwhile, Wandua, the only person to have last seen the goat, was on a desperate mission a half-day walk away, to woo back his wife from her parents. He was to arrive with his wife that afternoon, and it was in the euphoria of a second chance by his beloved wife that the news about the goat greeted them. He wasted no time and headed straight for Grandmother Munira's homestead.

The Grandmother had kindly thanked him for taking the trouble to bring her the important bit of information, and together they had set out for Kamau's homestead. The purposefulness in her aged step told it all, and need not have bothered to explain to passers-by what it was all about. So word got around, and even as she entered Kamau's clattered homestead, a crowd had begun to gather.

The surprise on Kamau's face could not hide his guilt. It was not unlike that of villain complacent in his imagined invincibility, for he was caught most unawares. Still, if indeed he was the culprit, there needed more tangible evidence. And there it lay, in broad daylight for everyone to see. It was spread on his fence to dry in the afternoon sun—the unmistakable hide of Mareka, the goat!

Ah, the crowd went mad. All those years of pent-up anger at the slippery Kamau, who had now locked himself in his hut, found their vent that moment. Shouts of "lynch him! Finish him!" rent the air and within no time his fence was down. The hut in which he hid they could have easily brought down, if they didn't torch it and smoke him out like a stubborn bee and exact their long deferred revenge which, in their morbid anger, could have been as sweet as honey.

But they didn't! For between the hut and the crowd in all her frailty was Grandmother Munira, who standing erect had stretched her brittle bones and wailed in that thin, shaky voice of the aged, "Over my dead body! Nobody— Nobody dare touch him! The goat was mine and I forgive him!"

Well, the rest is history, and suffice it to say that Kamau was to live to see another day. He is a changed man now but Grandmother Munira and her goat have since become legendary. Indeed, you might often hear accounts of this incident around cooking fires in the evening by mothers instructing their attentive children. You might hear them draw a moral from it saying, "Forgiveness, along with other virtues, like Grandmother Munira's, means only one thing— sacrifice."

CROSSING THE 'I'

JANE WANJA MADE her way home to the village of Kimata. It was far yet, but the distance was shorter than the way she had come. There were few thoughts on her mind, and neither could she bear to think of the place nor the life she had come from. It was too painful to remember. This she had conveniently blotted out of her mind. And to confirm this, she carried nothing of that life except the clothes she had on.

If asked about it, she would have vaguely answered, "I was a woman of the world." Pressed to clarify, she probably would have replied, "if you must know, I was a courtesan," or perhaps she would have said, "an hostess," before nonchalantly adding, "never mind where." But one need no genius to divine that she was a prostitute. Even so, what might have led her there? She might have answered, "This or that reason. A thousand reasons, what does it matter?" Thus would have ended this unsatisfactory conversation. And now Jane was on her way home.

It was in nature's indiscriminating grace, however, that the greenery bordering her path helped her forget that dark past. The sun shone on the scattered trees and shrubs, which were beautifully interspersed with grass and a motley of wild flowers that grow in the plains. All of which in unison seemed to thankfully release a fragrance only she could enjoy. And the birds, happily chattering from their lofty homes, seemed to agree.

All these Jane took in appreciatively. As she looked about herself, as if to ascertain that she was indeed going home, a flower caught her eye —a daisy. The memory it evoked caught her most unawares.

She remembered that day when she was seven years old. She had been by a stream near her home. And a short distance downstream was a bridge that passers-by used on their way to Kimai or Rurii in either direction. It however was not used much for there was a shorter route on the other side of the ridge. They had agreed with her two friends, Wanjira and Wairimu, to meet there that morning to gather reeds to make dolls. But either she had been too early or they had taken long in their coming, for Jane had decided to gather reeds on her own as she waited for them. And knowing they would show up any minute, she kept looking towards the bridge, for that was the way they were bound to use, since their respective homes were near each other in the direction of Kimai not far from the stream.

It was while glancing towards the bridge that she noticed the stranger. For how long he had stood there watching her she could not tell, but the stranger had smiled and approached her. Jane noticed he was rather short and slim, and walked with hunched shoulders. He wore a shaggy beard and his hair was also unkempt. Other than that, he carried a small bag and wore a bright yellow robe and walked bare feet. All told, Jane had decided he was not exactly a handsome man. But what had struck her most about this stranger was the deep kindness she felt in him. She had liked him immediately.

"Good morning, little girl," the stranger had greeted her with a humility she could not understand.

"Good morning, sir," she had greeted him back.

"I think I am lost ," he had explained, inquiring, "Could you direct me to Rurii?"

Jane had been to Rurii many times, and hesitating only for a moment, she had explained to the stranger how to get there the best way she could before concluding, "But it is very far from here."

"Thank you. Thank you very much," the stranger had profused his gratitude, which only served to disarm the little girl.

Then, pointing at the stream, he humbly asked, "Could I please have a drink of water?"

This asking for her permission had greatly surprised Jane, and not knowing how or whether to reply, she had said nothing. Nevertheless her curiosity at this stranger increased as he bent to scoop water with his hands. His thirst finally quenched, even more surprised was Jane as he said "Thank you" again wiping his mouth contentedly. But feeling herself unworthy of the stranger's gratitude, she modestly said, "Everybody uses this water, sir. You don't have to thank me."

"No, I don't," the stranger replied with a smile, "but you have been kind enough to excuse me have my fill. You could have continued picking the reeds, but you didn't. You waited for me. Do you understand me?"

Jane said nothing. She still didn't think she had done anything to merit the stranger's gratitude.

Seeing her obvious incomprehension, the stranger had then looked about them, and spotting a patch of dry ground he said to Jane, "Come, let me explain."

She had unquestioningly followed as the

stranger handed her a stick he had picked from the ground. And squatting on the dry patch, he said to Jane who had remained standing , "Write the letter 'I' in the dust."

This she did, but the stranger said, "No, not the small 'i' - capital 'I'."

"The big 'I'?" Jane asked, for this is how she knew it as she had been taught in school.

The stranger nodded, and this she wrote.

"Now," the stranger instructed, "cross the 'I'."

But the girl, not comprehending, asked, "How?"

The stranger thought for a moment then replied, "By putting a dash across it."

After this was done, he asked, "Now, what sign have you made?"

"A plus?" the girl replied uncertainly.

"Yes, a plus," the stranger agreed. "That is what you have just done by the stream. You crossed the 'I'. You forgot yourself, that is, you momentarily forgot the importance the reeds had for you, and by that you added something by helping me solve my problem. That is why I am thanking you again."

This explanation had clearly been beyond Jane, and as this memory passed through her mind, she wondered why the stranger should have thought her able to understand him at that age. She however remembered that seeing her incomprehension the stranger had added encouragingly, "Well, never mind. You'll understand it someday. But always remember that."

But even as she remembered this, pausing only momentarily to recollect her thoughts, for some reason she conjured the village church in her imagination and discovered a new twist in the stranger's explanation.

"But this plus," she asked herself, "looked at differently, is it not a sign of the cross on a church steeple?" She understood the stranger now. Perfectly. And having been brought up a Christian, with the realization of the sign of the plus turning out to be a cross, the stranger's explanation had a tremendous impact on her. Incomplete biblical phrases like, "Love thy neighbour...," started coming to her mind. And as she continued thinking about it, she remembered having heard or read somewhere that "the cross was a heavy burden to bear." She understood it all now. And if the life she had led had taught her anything while mercilessly preying on men to survive, it was that selflessness was difficult if not impossible. But suddenly, this was now the cross she had to bear with all her conviction.

This feeling, this uplifting realization, was a new and inexplicable experience she had no words to describe. Yet she wondered whether the stranger himself was a Christian. She thought not, but decided he was a religious man all the same. And as this memory of the stranger lingered, she remembered that they had talked for a little while longer about themselves when the stranger explained to her that names don't always mean much, and that she should only call him her friend. And when time came from him to leave, he had walked to where there was growing some flowers and picked a daisy. This he had stuck on Jane's hair and said words that, recalling them now, made her feel good about herself again. He had said as he bid her good-bye:

> To nick-name you Daisy
> Is to sing in the hearts
> I've known to relish
> Your noble freshness
>   And temper
> Their own to grow fuller
> In a portrait that counts
>   For beauty—You
> Count for Beauty.

The stranger had then left, leaving imprints of his bare feet on the ground.

Her two friends, Wanjira and Wairimu, arrived a short while later. But in their childish patter about the dolls they were going to make, the memory of the stranger had been forgotten among the reeds.

Jane was twenty-eight-years-old now, and feeling herself a new person, she wondered what became of her two childhood friends. She sighed knowing that she would find out soon enough.

She walked unhurriedly yet purposefully, and the village waited where the stranger's words and her faith in them, steeped in hope and fortitude, would blossom like the daisy that was once stuck on her hair.

DAWN, FATHER AND I

Society. Money. Art. The first craves.
The second provides. The third remembers,
weeps and hopes or cues an age.

I DON'T CLAIM to understand St Valentine's day, but recalling it a few years ago I am not without mirth that even fate does not lack in sense of humour. While it may be common knowledge that this day is for the romantic to express his love, I have ever marvelled at the coincidence that it was the one I was forced, instead, to task in explication of my indulgence in art, my only love. Yet which artist could explain his love for art? Which lover his love? No matter.

The day had started as casually as any other and would have ended uneventful and tranquil had it not been for that evening. I was in my studio where I was in excitement labouring to capture a lead into one of those creative insights that happen on the spur of the moment. With me was Dawn who was seated by the bookshelf leafing through one of her numerous magazines.

Now, it was this excitement that was to mark the beginning of what was to follow. Yet whether it was this she had sensed in me I can not tell, but I had suddenly felt her gaze on me and when I looked up she said, "You know I look at you and don't see success."

That remark took me with such a jolt of surprise that whatever it was that was the cause of my excitement I completely forgot. My mouth turned dry, and at a loss of what to make of the remark, did not know how to respond.

This was not a light sentiment to be put into words, even by a fourteen-year-old who had continued, as if to give me a cue. "Come now," she said, "you know what I am talking about." Then with that strange, slangy know-it-all manner of the teenager, rapped, "Of course, there's no juice in wooing up the pen."

Now I don't begrudge the poetic sensibilities of teenage, but to put her words in more civil language, what she meant was that one did not just grow rich by taking up writing, referring to my budding career. She had a point, of course, but to appreciate the essence of this disquieting preamble to the ensuing incident, allow that I digress a bit in order to introduce my family as it was up until then.

I was twenty one years old then, and other than being seven years my younger, Dawn, a fresh faced girl, uninhibited and eager as they come, was also my only sibling in the surviving family of three that included Father. Mother had long left us "breath unbound" during the difficult birth of Dawn, who had been born prematurely in a seeming impatience to get into this world.

I can't say I remember much of Mother except that she had an arboreal patch she cultivated in our ample yard. Here I remember we spent much of our time with her and Father such that in the words of her favourite song, we were "One among the trees and the stars in the sky, sighing with the whispering birds, serene on the towering trees..."

That is the snatch of memory which to remember brings to mind her wrenching departure that changed my world. This was especially so because immediately after her departure, Father, in his grief, had assumed a paternity so zealous for his newly born daughter that while I can boast of having been Mama's boy, Dawn was certainly Father's girl. I have often wondered what Mother would have thought of this, for this was suddenly a new Father to me. A Father I could no longer relate to.

In my seven-year-old mind I could not realize it then, but that was where our estrangement took its insoluble root. In his peculiar fixation with Dawn he daily lived the very moment of her birth, so that his life seemed frozen in the fact. I don't know how else to put it, but it was not unlike the sovereign or court of arms persists engraved on a coin, for, indeed he was that very coin! And in his complacent wealth, the future held no sway. It was a promise vague in its vastness – for Dawn, whom it seemed he solely existed playing host to her every whim so that she literally ran him, and therefore the family.

You must forgive me if I liken that sister of mine to the gods, but the Father I speak was most certainly her own invention. As for me I was her batten but melancholy elder brother who was content to be in her shadow as far as Father was concerned.

Dawn and I were very close, however, and in her position between me and Father it was she who held the family together. So I must admit to her charisma, and a fascination she held for me that had inspired many a portrait in my work. These she appreciated and in her teenage vanity craved more of. Her feelings for me were therefore indubitable, for while I preferred solitude, at least to keep away from her often constricting ambit, she tirelessly sought my company for the sake of it, just so that we could be together. And thus we were in my studio on the evening of that St. Valentine's day.

Therefore, that I had always assumed her sympathy in my work, the more surprising her remark about success had come to me. But there was no gainsaying the fact that because of Father, and no doubt her magazines, success to her was a simple pecuniary equation.

Recovering from the initial reaction to her remark, I was suddenly seized by a desperate urge to explain — explain why I was an artist. Why I was who I was. The thought that had spurred this urge to explain was this; "Is it not that relationships risk disintegration if invariably unstoked, even those between siblings? Or in their dynamism, is it not a fact that relationships need justification time and again in order to thrive?" Whatever the answer. But at that moment it dawned on me that she had never understood me, and, to my horror, neither had I. It was going to be as much a self justification as it was going to be a baring of my soul to Dawn.

This was hardly a happy thought, for what was I going to explain to her? What? All I knew was I had to explain, somehow. It was not unlike the urge I knew so well. An urge that gnaws my insides for relief, growing steadily to a singular high that wracks my whole self. This feeling always came after what I can only call gestation, even for a fraction of a second, of an artistic child whose time had come. And the time to explain and justify myself had come, though I had never really thought of it until that moment. This realization was forbidding, for I had the terrible feeling that the result this would derive was going to weaken or even break whatever bond there was between us. But what had to be done, had to be done.

I must have lapsed into one of my long contemplative silences she only knew too well, for when I finally looked at her she had reverted to glossing through her magazine.

"Dawn," I had then called her name but she apparently didn't hear. "Dawn," I called again and she looked up. "You don't understand," I said hoping her response would help formulate what needed to be said.

"What?" she asked rather nonchalantly and this lethargic response provoked in me such a sense of anger that I didn't even need to think, for an idea suddenly possessed my mind.

"Art...," I began to say, but at that very moment Father walked into the studio cutting me short. It almost seemed as if he had been larking behind the door waiting for just that.

His first words were, "Ah, the word!" as if I had just uttered some obscenity. Then he asked in his characteristically beautiful and appealing yet detached tone, "Am I interrupting something?"

"Oh, no—no," I hastily replied and in my lie hoped he would leave immediately because his presence was not going to help matters with Dawn.

But he just stood there uncertainly, as he glanced questioningly at Dawn who then said as if to answer the unasked question, "I was just telling him," she gestured vaguely at me, "that the stuff he is doing won't get him anywhere in the end." Then she stated, "With his brains he could do better—much better."

"Better, indeed," echoed Father as he pulled a chair to sit down.

"And to imagine," Dawn continued, " he pretends to be happy, penniless—"

Father shook his head at this in wonder, or perhaps to affirm her disbelief, as the last word was left hanging in the air.

Now that it was clear Father was here to stay, I had no illusions it was by design. I wondered whether it was by design too that I was being discussed like I was miles away. "You don't understand," I said not knowing how else to respond but also to assert my presence.

"Now who doesn't understand here?" retorted Dawn indignantly. "You are penniless, and that's a fact," she spat out disparagingly.

I didn't blame her. The fault lay in Father's presence in which time and again, like a spoilt child, Dawn seemed a diabolic angel, confident in the havoc she could wreak as Father looked on with a pensive eye.

Fearing things were decidedly getting nasty even before they had began, I took the initiative and adopted a different direction. "The way you are looking at it," I said imputing some kind of logic, "take the penniless result of my work as an occupational hazard..."

Instead of responding they both stared at me as if I had suddenly gone insane.

I continued, "My contentment, though, is that

you appreciate my work."

"Yes, I do," Dawn agreed, and stealing a glance at Father in an obvious signal, she said, "But this is what I really enjoy," and she waved her magazine at me.

"I am offering you a job at the magazine—all options and all found," said Father, suddenly animated in his appealing voice which was strangely beautiful in its curious blend of rustling paper and grating metal. Among his many business interests, he owned, or rather published a glossy magazine that catered to rich socialites like Dawn.

But how to put it? That though I did not deny he was who he was, I could not work for the magazine? That I could not accept him, his ethic— profit, and be the same person I was? Never mind I had little inkling of who I was, which was my hope to find out with Dawn before he came in.

Not wishing to hurt his feelings, I ignored replying to his offer directly and reached for the magazine which I leafed through pretending to make up my mind.

Then I said to Dawn referring to the magazine, "This assault of form and colour in your eye that is still the music in your ear, the sweet in your tongue as it is the rose in your breath..."

"Now, if that is not art!" cried Dawn with that uncertain enthusiasm of one trying to make out whether what she had heard was what was really meant.

"No," I wanted to reply, "in its superficiality it is nothing more than a commodity." Instead I said, surprising myself because it was purely involuntary, "Real art is that and more: it is the paint that steals the content in your eye to reach, nay, exalt the sublime self within. Or, put another way, the artist's brush-strokes are the throes of The Soul denuded."

I don't know how I must have sounded, but provoked a bewildered "interesting" from Dawn before Father filled in the silence that followed by asking, "But what do you mean? Are you taking up on my offer or are you not?"

Before I could answer, Dawn, in her all knowing manner, misunderstanding that I had not accepted the offer, explained my "immortal" fault to Father. "I have never known an artist," she said, "who was not an egoist; a kind of god who the world did not revolve around..."

Now, I guess it was the tone in which she said this, or perhaps I resented the obvious lack of respect for me, yet it might have been that word "god", but incensed I retorted cutting her short, "A piece of art is no less edifying than God is spiritual!"

Maybe this remark was irrelevant, yet I clearly see it now I probably meant to say that in my lonely labours I did not mean to be an egoist, it is that my result need be pristine from unfathomable depths in my intention, no matter the subject, to bring forth the very same unrelieved yet exhilarating primordial being in every one of us—but I digress.

"Spiritual," Father repeated. "I suppose to you that is how affective your, er, work is, huh?! Poppycock!" he swore. "The truth," he went on, "is that you are out in the cold in that you have no money yet you know very well there's something we can do about that."

Hearing him say this, a certain sadness enveloped me for no matter how noble his intentions seemed, there was still the unspoken fact that I would be giving up myself or, more precisely, selling myself short.

"I appreciate your concern," I replied, "but that truth is your truth." I wanted to add that whatever his truth, the Truth is like a light switch in a room that was no more responsible for its being than it was for the darkness surrounding it; that art was probably one way of turning it on. But such ideas, like the one of God, are just that and take imagination to breath which Father was not up to, given his decided indifference to the arts. So I said, "I am not in the cold, as you put it. I want for nothing. And as of how my work affects me, it is precisely that you are seated here dousing a nonexistent fire. I don't need a job."

I had finally given my answer, but I couldn't have anticipated the reaction. The atmosphere in the studio suddenly grew tense and cold, and in her disbelief, Dawn, who in her hurt suddenly looked her age, gazed up at Father seeking courage and support as she incredulously asked, "What!"

That is when Father exploded. "Who the hell are you to..." The rest of his tirade I can not put into words. All I can say is that the most charitable of his sentiments was that I was "some childish imbecile who ought to know better!"

Maybe so. But I was gripped by such a sadness that I choked with emotion when I wondered where one might really go wrong to have a legitimate choice and seek to live it. Even as this went through my mind, there was this unremitting stream of words I could not tame to coherence. It went like this, "You are one...of a freedom... that...

behooves... a responsibility... to purge... yet... gratify the heart with as much... beauty... as to reflect...in repoussé...the wayward...in trying to amend for the follies of..." It kept repeating itself over and over in my mind like the spark of a poem seeking to be thrashed out on paper, only that I could not pursue it in the compromised situation I was languishing in.

It was not unusual to have words or images pass through my mind when I was in distress, but when relief came it always struck most suddenly. This was such a case, and the realisation that came to me was in a flash: That, masquerading as individuals, the ironies in which we live as social beings preclude the mirror our ingenuity exhibit about ourselves. I had no better way of putting it, but how simple everything seemed then! I had found myself, at least partly, because I was not sure I could explain why I was an artist. Yet how to tell Dawn with Father there that I was who I was because they were precisely who they were!

It was then that I started weeping at the futility of it all when I heard Dawn ask, her voice seeming to come from a great distance, "Now what has got into him?"

I wished to reply but marvelled instead at what

a purging experience crying can be. For, as in such emotional outbursts that leave the mind surprisingly lucid, it became clear to me that in her immaturity she held the promise like that of even the darkest of nights, that, somewhere yonder larked a new Dawn, and aware of it or not, she would come to her own when her time was up. It was then it occurred to me with absolute certainty that no matter the outcome of what had transpired that evening, mine was to keep that promise steeped in its splendour before her path.

With this realization a strange calm came over me. And as Father rose from his chair I forgave his cynicism when he uttered "Ah, the word!" when he entered the studio. It was then the first lines of this short poem, which I will recite in passing, started forming in my mind:

> Art! There's a word
> You'll never hurl
> With a clenched fist
>
> A word rinsed of flesh
> As it is a child of Muse
> Borne of the appointed heart
> Spelling art - art

A word freeing the eye
In a flight
No bird ever flies

A word in eternal bloom

"Let's go," muttered Father to Dawn, and a look I had come to know clouded his eyes—a look which always seemed to say that I was his son but a different son.

As the door closed behind them, Dawn cast a lingering look at me so that Father commented, "He is too emotional for anyone's good."

Thus I was left, alone, an eccentric who had to be tolerated.

But what I would have liked to tell Dawn then, as now, is that perhaps there is nothing like success to the artist. Whatever that is, it resides in the spectator who perceives it as such. Financial reward is not success, it is an enabling environment merely, not an end. Yet success, if such be the word, for the artist is the act of finally capturing that tiny fragment at once within yet without all possible imagination, whatever be his reason, including Beauty. That, and, needless to add, the day lives not forever except in art, perhaps.

THE D-WORD

THERE ARE THOSE life stories we often hear being told in four words: "From rags to riches." Stories that in their fleeting narrative seem adequate, even magical, despite the stark reality of those men and women they tell about. All told, however, their finer details make for a rather coarse texture, as often revealed by the difficult path of their valiant subjects to success.

Yet it is not these stories that are worth talking about, it is their triumphant lot, among whom there occurs a rare breed; a man I once met in the line of duty. His life story, though of the few word variety to boot, was somewhat more ambitious. It read thus, as I found it etched in stone at his residence:

THE D-WORD

dreams' & desires' denouement
diligently developed
determine debonair daylights

Now, for the moment, without bothering to explain the above curiosity, I must keep my word and not reveal it's author's identity. All I can say is that he is a highly developed individual, an inveterate philanthropist and a meliorist. And that he is the founder of a conglomerate that manufactures anything from hand held fans to jet turbines. An enterprise that in his many inscrutabilities he had requested me to give a single but apt name, INDUSTRY.

Anyway, that is "the happy ending in my story," as he had put it to me. At which point he had also asked me not to reveal his name or the details of his simple and reclusive life.

But what made the middle of his story, which was the reason I had tirelessly sought for his interview, for a business article in order to quote his excellent example to prospective entrepreneurs?

This had been his confounding reply. "On waking, dream and all, then blossom, all in the D-word."

My question, to put it another way, had been unnecessary for all there was to know about the middle of his story he had already told—in The D-Word.

"But if you must quote my example," he had however continued, "mine is to say that one must never cease to dream. I am whoever wants to be, for, of our achievements, are we not our dreams and desires crafted true? To that I have little doubt, and the path blazes in the D-word. Yet I wish to emphasise that I am no different from anybody else, for in this pursuit of ourselves you find that the middle and ending in each of our stories is similar to tens of thousands of others. It is the beginning of each that is personal – deeply personal."

Well. I must confess that I never came to write the article, for I had little to go on other than what he had just said. But also because to put his name down as "Mr So and So" in the manner of our journalistic pretensions, adding, "Not his real name", seemed rather disrespectful. Still, neither would his story have "washed" in the eyes of my policy encumbered editors anyway.

So having put down the middle of his story, which he admitted was a ringing account of unrelenting hard work (diligently developed), and its ending in "debonair daylights", which perhaps in his success alludes to his essence and character in his good if anonymous deeds to the society, I now proceed to narrate the "deeply personal" moment of his beginning as he literally relived it for my curious benefit. I say "literally" because it was such that even without telling me more than he thought I should know, I saw it unfold almost as if I was in his mind as it happened when he was only a boy...

He was thirteen years old then. And that day he was in the hut nursing the Aged One who for some months had been bed-ridden. Outside, as he could gauge the weather through the tiny window, there was that thin rain that showers intermittently with the sun still shining, giving the landscape an unconvincing quality. But it was oppressively hot in the hut and every now and then he would use a handkerchief to mop away beads of sweat that kept forming on the Aged One's forehead. When he was not doing this, in his hands was a flat pan they used to cover the cooking pot with, and with which he was awkwardly fanning the Aged One to keep her cool.

The pan was uncomfortable to use however, given its sharp and jagged edges, and that it kept slipping from his sweaty hands. So he vainly sought for an easier way to go about the fanning. But even as he stoically bore himself to the necessity of having to use it, some not unpleasant sensations on his hands kept intruding into his mind. It was the sixth finger on each of his hands, as these extra digits rhythmically flopped this way and that in a seeming therapeutic dance of some kind accompanying his fanning.

He could not explain why but a certain fondness for them seemed to overwhelm him, something he never imagined he'd ever feel for them because he hated his hands with all his heart. So, like one testing the validity of this alien feeling that was pervading his being, he let his mind wander in recollection of the unhappy memories that nature in its malice, endowing him with these unnecessary fingers, had wrought him.

As the memories came flooding in, it occurred to him that for as long as he could remember he had been subject to childish ridicule among his peers. And recalling some of the instances when he was around them, he might hear somebody quip, "How does one greet a six fingered hand?" and there would follow that agonizing laughter of sarcasm among its childish respondents. Or there might be a game going on involving counting and someone else might sarcastically suggest, "Let him count, he owns like a thousand fingers," and the same dreadful laughter would again follow. Or again he might hear another one say with mock indignation, referring to the extra fingers' helpless and uncontrollable pointing, "Tell him to stop pointing at me!"

Such might have been innocent if puerile jokes, but their memory so vividly haunted him that even as he fanned the Aged One he could hear the hollow laughter still ringing in his ears. They were the pain he knew; the very fact that he was different from his peers. Of this, he particularly remembered one instance when he was six years old.

He and four of his slightly older friends had gathered to play a game in which two players held out a hand each and intertwined their fingers with an object to extricate at least one finger from the other's grip. It was a consuming game of hand strength and had only one rule, that, other than the thumbs no other finger should remain free when the tussle began.

He had always enjoyed watching this game being played but being a little self-conscious of his six fingered hands he had never participated in it. This was going to be his first time. But just before the game was set to begin an argument had started. And in their logic, the other four players argued that since he had six fingers to a hand against their five (of which they had shown him their hands to emphasise the point as if he didn't already know) it would leave one finger of his hand free, which was clearly against the game's cardinal rule. Never mind that it was obvious the finger in question was of no practical value in any kind of situation that requires the use of hands. But on that technicality he had to be eliminated from playing.

The pain he felt then was such as he had never felt before. Blind with tears and unable to protest as deep emotion gripped at his throat in a thick knot of dejection, he never waited to see how the game would progress. From then on he had few friends among his peers, and neither did he ever witness another of that game.

Therefore while he had grown used to being alone when he was not with the Aged One, he had also grown to hate his hands. And many were the times he held a knife undecided whether to cut off the extra fingers whose very presence had taken the form of physical pain anytime he touched or even looked at them. Thus his serious doubts that they were not a pain any more but a pleasurable pair of frenzied dancers in tune with his fanning.

After this, something seemed to have opened up inside him, for like one discovering a friend he never thought he had, he was gripped by a sudden urge to examine them. He stopped in his fanning, wiped a bead of sweat from the Aged One's forehead, then stared fascinatedly at his hands. Looking at them he thought the extra fingers stuck out rather proudly, and it occurred they were telling him something the message of which he somehow connected with the pan on his lap.

In the absurdity of the thought he found himself involuntarily spreading the other fingers, stiffening them as if in comparison, when an idea he could not quite grasp came and went in an instant and a certain inexplicable thrill ran through his body.

At that very moment, the Aged One opened her eyes and smiled as if she too had experienced the same inexplicable thrill. Then, to his consternation, like one summarizing his past in fortification for some mysterious future, the Aged one said between laboured breaths, "The joys in life don't always matter, it is the pains we endure that make it worth living." Then she closed her eyes again with a contented look on her face.

He immediately forgot about his preoccupations

with his hands and wondered whether the Aged
One was not in one of those deliriums that hadn't
visited her in a long time. Yet, how startling the
irony in her utterance when he thought of the pains
she daily went through, forgetting the pains he
himself had known. Though he could not
understand it, he could not dare ask her to explain,
lest he excite her from her serene convalescence
as suddenly reflected on her wizened face. But
whatever she had meant she was not a pain to him,
nor was she a burden.

He looked back to the time when the Aged One
had the stroke that was to render her invalid. He
was only eight years old and overnight he had
turned from being child and ward to being
guardian and provider. It was then he had started
fending for both of them, including procuring her
expensive medication. But those past few months
it had happened that she could no longer walk on
her own and had to lie on her straw-bed helpless.
Then he had to start dividing his time between her
and working—whether tilling, weeding or
harvesting their better endowed neighbours'
land—for money. But neither of all this was a
pain to him. And though he had never thought of
it, it suddenly occurred to him that all he ever did

was for the Aged One. And, come to think of it, he felt that she was indeed his only joy.

On this happy thought he tenderly cast a monitoring eye at the Aged One who looked comfortable enough, then his mind was back to his hands again. But compelled by some unforthamable urge he spoke quite involuntarily, for it was not his intention to disturb the Aged One.

"Aged One," he said, "I am going to make a fan that is easier to use than this pan."

And to his surprise he realised that what he had just said was indeed the idea that a moment ago had come and gone in an instant. An idea that nevertheless didn't surprise him for it seemed he had always known that was what he would end up doing.

It was so real in his mind that looking at his hands he could clearly visualise his fingers (including the extra two which added to a peculiarly beautiful patterning) as the ribs that supported the paper or cloth that made the fan. He even visualised that as his fingers closed together so did the fan, such that it could fit in a pocket.

This vision of the fan grew and he clearly saw

people with money in their hands clamouring for it full of wonder at its innovativeness. Then, somehow because of the fan, he saw the Aged One up and about again, free and full of vigour just like she was before her ailment.

"Aged One," he called her name unable to contain his excitement. "Aged One, I am going to make...Aged One!" He stopped suddenly shouting the name in shocked disbelief. "Aged One!" He called her again, this time in a strangled wail.

But the Aged One was past hearing as her strange stillness testified with numbing eloquence. Yet she looked serene, even beautiful. Yet again, just like in the vision of the fan, all he could see now in quick succession was the empty straw-bed that was now the mound of soil by the side of the hut, that was now the Aged One's last words which he wore like an armour, that was now the difficult path on which he now trod in making the fan that would lead him to riches as etched in the D-Word.

ADAN

YOU KNOW MY FRIEND Boru Jattani. What you probably may not know is that Boru is the son of a former nomad who at one time roamed the arid wilderness of North Eastern province of Kenya, but had settled with his family at a more westerly location towards the middle of the country at a place called Garba Tulla, in Eastern Province. Here Boru started his education and went on to become a lecturer in Linguistics at our local college, as you well know.

Well, he recently invited me to this place of his childhood. But no longer having a home there (his parents had moved to Isiolo where he has built them a home) we were to camp by a dried remnant of what was once a thriving shrub.

"The weather can be very atrocious here," Boru had explained, referring to the shrub as we put up our tent.

Now, it was the tone in which he said this that first got me wondering whether it was a coincidence that we were camping at that particular spot. Until that moment, being a nature lover, I had accompanied him to "savour," as he had put it, "the beauty of arid Kenya." But somehow the shrub now seemed to allude a whole new dimension to it.

"Might I be misplaced in feeling that this shrub means something to you," I had asked as we tied the last knot to the tent.

Boru didn't answer immediately. He looked distantly at the twisted acacia trees around us, which unlike the shrub seemed to have borne well the weather, then looked at the sandy soil and pursing his lips, he quoted lines I had completely forgotten about.

He said,

"In childhood, wonder.
In ripe age, wisdom.
The one, the root.
The other, the fruit.

There-in, in either,
Look for heaven."

I remembered that these lines I had jotted unpremeditated on a paper napkin in a bar in response to some argument or other I had had with Boru. But even as I recollected this, my good friend was saying, "Yes. The shrub means something to me. It once constituted my 'heaven.'" It seemed I had provoked one of those memories that one shares only with those most close to him. And fancying myself close to Boru, which until then I had never even thought about, I said, "I am curious. Want to share it?"

Again Boru didn't answer immediately. And while, as I imagined, he made up his mind whether I merited the description, "a close friend," I busied myself with fixing us a cool drink which we needed after the work we had just completed in the afternoon heat.

I handed him his drink and as we moved into the coolness of the tent, Boru said, "Makes me feel like a child again to tell it."

Indeed, he was to go on and tell it with unbridled juvenile enthusiasm that grew bolder with every word, such that at some point he might have been a child telling it. This is what he related to me.

"You need no introduction to my family history," Boru began. "Now, we had settled some four or so miles to the north of what is now Garba Tulla High School (it was not in existence then, but it is the school I pointed out to you on our way here). This is the distance I had to traverse every morning and evening to and from a now extinct primary school that used to be in close proximity to the location where the high school now stands.

"But I can't talk about the shrub without mentioning the path I took in my solitary journeys to and from school. Like most paths it zigzagged its way around a bolder here, a thorny bush there, or even one of those massive though corroded ant-hills which you might have noticed dot this countryside. Due to its many turns it always seemed to me a wonder that it kept this course, and I woke up every morning with a burning desire to use it, at least, in order to catch the dew that would be waiting for my bare feet to beat. Of this I had formed a certain attachment to the path which seemed there only for me, waiting, before the unforgiving sun could rise and dry the dew on it.

"But the path always had other things waiting for me, like the ever green shrub, now pathetic and dead as you can see.

"In its splendour it always was a sight to behold. To begin with, it was so large that it looked like a leafy, thick branched tree without a trunk. On it inhabited various kinds of insects, birds and creeping plants. It was unlike any other I had seen or anybody else, for that matter, for no one seemed to have a name for it.

"I can not begin to explain my fascination with the shrub, but, as you need not to be told, mine was that age of innocence— that age of curiosity where apprehension, in every sense of the word, one is wrapped in infinite wonder at nature and its schemes. So as you might imagine many were the times I sat by the path after school just to observe the activity on the shrub. This, such that I had come to know it by heart - every branch and creeping tendril, the countless nests and, I fancied, every bird, bee and butterfly that depended on it.

"Yet it is not these things that keep the shrub most in my mind, it is an acquaintance I made one bright afternoon when I was eight.

"I had just reached the shrub on my way home from school when I perceived a certain change. Perhaps it was that I knew the shrub so well that if there was a change I would most certainly sense it. I was to confirm this a few moments later when I noticed something scramble from a large nest, which was sort of flat shaped like a plate, that had laid hidden in the deeply shadowed parts of the shrub. I was certain that it had not been there in the morning, nor the small animal with the bushy tail, brownish-yellow in colour, that I saw scramble from it and disappear to the other side of the shrub.

"It had all happened so fast that, startled, I could not tell what sort of animal it was. In fact, I was about to run as fast as I could, fearing it was a dangerous animal, when to my surprise it showed its face as if spying on me. It was a squirrel. Seeing this I relaxed a little because I had never heard of squirrels attacking people. Still, one never knew with animals.

"I decided to be friendly and started making queer noises with my mouth as I imagined it would make, all this while ready to run in case it mistook my intentions. But nothing happened. The squirrel just stood there eyeing me curiously.

"It was then I remembered a friend of mine with whom I had to be separated when my family had to settle. His name was Adan, and I thought the squirrel looked a bit like him. Even as I thought this, I whispered the name when an idea occurred to me.

"I was going to make the squirrel my friend and if he agreed I was going to name him after Adan. To this end I scoured the bottom of my lunch pouch, which was attached on the inside of my schoolbag, and came up with a few morsels of food. These I waved in a manner to suggest that they were food and I intended no harm. Then I hurled one bit in front of him. But still suspicious, the squirrel remained where he was. I made my queer noises again while softly telling him to eat the food and threw him another morsel. That did it, for the squirrel edged from behind the shrub to the food. He then sat on his hind legs and held the food with his fore-limb as squirrels do and ate it.

"'Adan,' I called softly and by that name I came to know him from that day on.

"Adan, the squirrel, seemed to like my food because immediately he was through with the first morsel he took the other and ate it, then looked at me as if begging for more. I let the squirrel have another as I spared one in my hand. After he was through with it I let him see the remaining one in my hand and held it out for him to eat. He did, and I knew then that we had become friends.

"Then, to confirm this as a seal of our friendship, Adan did a most surprising thing. He scrambled to his nest and came back with a red berry which he placed at my feet. I picked it up and briefly examined it then put it in my pocket. I was to carry it with me for many days after that before it finally shrivelled. But it could not germinate when I planted it.

"Anyway, after accepting Adan's gift I ran around in a playful manner, and understanding what I was doing Adan ran with me in the same fashion. After this I ran into the open field with him close at my heels, as if he was chasing me and I evading capture. We played these little games for a long time that it was almost dark before I realized it was late.

"'It is time to go now,' I said to Adan not knowing how else to bid him good-bye. 'But wait for me in the morning as I go to school.' Then I walked away.

"But when I looked back, there was Adan following me. I stopped and he came right to where I was standing and I bent to stroke his fur.

"'Okay,' I said, 'If you want to come home with me, that's fine, but I don't know how mother will take it. Anyway, you come —I'll find a place where you can hide.'

"Then I set off again and he followed. I don't know for how long we walked like this but after some time I noticed that Adan had stopped. I knew then he would not come with me.

"'Bye,' I said, 'see you in the morning. Don't forget.'

"I went home fingering the berry in my pocket that Adan had given me, hoping to find him at the shrub when I passed by there in the morning. That night I dreamt of nothing but Adan, the squirrel.

"The next morning I woke up with great anticipation, because of Adan, of course. I removed the berry from under my pillow where I had kept it, fondled it, then put it my pocket. After readying myself for school, to my usual helping of lunch I added a little more for Adan. I wasn't sure he would remember me, and a little food, I reckoned, would jog his memory.

"How wrong I was, for as I approached the

shrub, in the distance I saw something moving towards me in rapid but awkward movement. It was Adan. I can't explain my joy at seeing him and I somehow knew that he would be with me for a long time. When he reached me he started strutting and running around me in a manner that told me that he too was happy to see me.

"'Hello, Adan,' I greeted him, then said, for he seemed to want to play, 'If we start to play now I'll be late for school, but I had brought you some food in case you had forgotten me.' I chuckled at this as I removed a handful of food from my schoolbag. I then extended my hand for him to take. Adan took the food with both his paws, took a bite, then holding the remainder with one paw he ran ahead of me in a most awkward manner, as if to make fun, so that I laughed. He was to stop a short distance ahead of me in the path while eating cheerfully as he waited for me to get to where he was. When I reached him I let him have the rest of the food on my palm and he did the same again running ahead of me and waiting. After this we went playing along the path. And for the first time for as long as I could remember I didn't even notice that we had passed the shrub until a while later.

"I wondered whether Adan would follow me to school and hoped not. His presence would not endear me to my teachers, let alone the interest Adan would generate with other children at school, some of whom would probably harm him. As if reading my unhappy thoughts, Adan suddenly stopped on his tracks, and what seemed a sad look in his eyes told me he would go no further.

"'Don't look so sad now,' I said in consoling tones as I explained, 'you see, in school I will be in class most of the time so we will have little time to play. But don't worry I'll be here in the evening again.'

"Then bidding him goodbye, I went to school. I wasn't to know it then but as time went on in our friendship, I started to notice that he had a certain distance he could not exceed from the shrub. This, to the effect that he always bid me good-bye at more or less the same spot in either direction on my way home or to school.

"I confirmed this one Saturday, which was not a school day, when I went visiting him. In our usual games, venturing into the thickets further than we had ever been from the shrub, I noticed Adan could go no further after a certain distance in any direction we extended our play. This distance was about three hundred meters from the shrub. The area within I took it to be his territory or something like that and therefore the only place we could play. But this had little effect in our joyous relationship day after day in my goings to and from school, or during holidays when I would spend more time with him. This, until one day when something happened.

"By now Adan had already come to know the time to expect me at the edge of his territory. Here also I had come to expect him waiting for me depending on where I was coming from on either side of the territory. So on this day I had woken up early as usual and readied myself for school. But on opening the door to get out of the house, to my great surprise, there he was right at our door step.

"'Adan!' I yelled his name, not even pausing to wonder how he had found my home. 'What are you doing here?' I asked as usual not expecting an answer.

"But on looking closer at him it became clear that this was not the usual jovial and playful Adan. Something was wrong. But what?

"'I sensed you are not happy' I said, then added 'whatever it is I am sure all will be well.' Then I motioned to him that we should be on our way.

"As we walked I noticed that, every now and then, Adan threw furtive glances around us, as if expecting trouble. I could sense his anxiety. But what was it that disturbed him so? If only he could talk, I thought to myself. These glances however increased as we neared the shrub which was far yet. Finally I said, just to calm him, 'I don't suppose I have done anything to hurt you. Or have I? As I recall yesterday we were as happy as ever as I taught you how to salute and match the way policemen do — left, right, left, right— remember?' But Adan was paying little attention as I continued, 'Then we shook hands as usual and bid each other good-evening...' As I said this, Adan changed from the anxiety I could only sense to visible panic.

"'Are you sick?' I asked as the panic increased. But Adan did what I could have least expected. All of a sudden he jumped in my path in a manner to suggest that he was barring me from walking on.

"'What are you doing, Adan!' I asked with alarm but he didn't respond. 'Something is terribly wrong here,' I thought to myself as I walked around him. Yet he shifted and still stood on my path.

"I stopped in my walking and said, 'If we continue like this I'll be late for school and that won't be nice.' Then I started on my way again. That's when he really got aggressive. He started biting at my feet so that I had no choice but to started kicking back as a I ran away from him. 'What does he want,' I asked myself bitterly because what struck me then was that we were really fighting each other, and the reason why, only Adan knew. It was very sad.

"When biting at my feet didn't stop me, Adan got more fierce and started tearing at my clothes as I fought back. Then, suddenly, he bit my hand and I dropped my school-bag. I bent down to pick it by the strap at which instant Adan grabbed the other side of the strap and started pulling me back towards the direction we had come. It was amazing. But also at that very instant I saw a movement that was almost imperceptible from the corner of my eye. I momentarily forgot about Adan and stopped to look. It was then, to my horror, everything became clear as to why Adan was behaving the way he was. He had all along been keeping me away from danger – indeed from a lion that stood by the shrub looking in our direction. It might have strayed from near the hills of Marsabit where I had heard there were wild animals, but I had no time to think about that.

"The lion was far yet, about a hundred or so metres from where I stood transfixed with fear. Now what was I going to do? I wondered. If I screamed nobody would hear me. My home was far behind, and the school further ahead, and nobody ever used the path so early in the morning. I was alone except perhaps for Adan who would be the only witness to what would happen: I would be torn to pieces right here and nobody to help me. I remembered all the good times I had had with the path, Adan, the shrub, my friends at school —all these passed through my mind. I felt sorry for my parents for the grief I'd cause them. Meanwhile, here I was face to face with the lion. Ah, but how I suffered in those moments.

"Little had I realized that Adan was now between me and the lion. His fur, in a way I had never noticed before, had so blended with the surroundings that it was almost impossible to spot him. He was inching ever so slowly towards the lion. What occurred to me then was that he was going to attack thus distract the lion from me, so that I could run for my life. But this was a selfish thought, I reprimanded myself; for what about Adan? What could he do against such a large animal? Just one bite in the lion's great jaws and it would be over for him, then it would be my turn. Even as these thoughts passed through my mind, Adan's fearlessness was a lesson to me, and feeling I couldn't let him down, I too summoned my courage and started thinking clearly.

"I had heard stories about the strength a lion was capable. But on that very word, 'strength', an idea on how to probably save the situation started forming in my mind. Animals sense fear, I remembered having heard that somewhere. So the first thing I did was not to show fear or even feel it. The next thing I remembered was that when two dogs, strange to each other, met, there was always one that wanted to dominate the other. And the stronger of the two kept a steady stare on the weaker one which would in its turn avert its eyes meekly to show submission, and with its tail between its legs would withdraw slowly backwards and run away.

"Now, I didn't think the lion would behave any different than dogs if I didn't make it feel threatened. As I averted my eyes to implement my plan, another thought entered my mind: Hungry lions tend to be aggressive. Was this one hungry? What if it attacked when I moved?

"I noticed that the distance between Adan and the lion had lessened considerably, yet the squirrel kept moving. But I also noticed that the lion's gaze was fixed on me so that it seemed not aware of Adan. I decided the time was now and moved slowly backwards and looking from the corner of my eyes, to my astonishment, I saw the lion move as well—backwards! But suddenly, as I made my next step backwards, Adan leaped in the air with a piercing cry that startled the lion. It's steady stare was trained on me and it had not noticed Adan's presence. The lion sprung and turned in the same instant and ran away in the opposite direction from me as I too turned and ran as fast as I could with Adan following me. We were safe.

When we stopped running the lion was nowhere to be seen. Adan, who was now behaving like my guardian, had his ears pricked with his eyes searching the distance. He went for my schoolbag where he had left it and handing it to me, he indicated in a way I can never explain that it was safe to go to school. This time he didn't bid me good-bye at the edge of his territory as usual, he went with me all the way to school always stopping and searching the distance to see whether the lion was after us.

"We arrived at school just after the bell had rang for classes. I had no doubt that he would enter the class with me, but he didn't and remained at the door. It wouldn't have mattered had the teacher inquired about him for I could have explained. But could anybody have believed me about what happened that morning? I don't know, but when the break-time came I looked for Adan who was nowhere to be seen. Knowing he had gone back to the shrub I could hardly wait for school to break up in the afternoon to meet him at the edge of his territory as usual. But he never was there when I came from school and neither was he at the shrub.

"I don't know what happened to him and I'll never know why he left, but that morning at the door to my class was the last I ever saw of Adan."

NDINGI'S RIDDLE

IT WAS AFTER DINNER and most of the other guests had told of their most memorable Christmas. Stories most of which were about how they met their first loves, some their husbands and wives, on Christmas eve at the village church. These they sweetened with the hilarious quarrels such amorous happenings often generate with jilted lovers. But they were getting a little monotonous, and when Ndingi's turn came he made a rather timely mistake of intimating that his story was "rather brief indeed", and had happened when he was six years old.

"Brief?" the host had wondered feigning surprise as he joked, "Seems to me like you want to cheat us off a good story." After a moment, with a hint of devilment playing in his eye, he had then suggested, "It will be most satisfactory, however, if the illustrious actor demonstrates his abilities by letting the six-year-old tell the story a week after it had happened? Wouldn't you agree, people?" And there had followed an amused applause, in complete agreement with the host.

It was all in comradely jest, of course, but the unfortunate Ndingi who was the only one of his kind in this amiable gathering, which incidentally also included a generous sprinkling of notable literati, wondered whether the host hadn't had a glass too many of his own excellent wine to misadvisedly assume actors to be necessarily of the same mould as playwrights. Whichever the case, he felt the host's suggestion rather unequal to his thespian abilities and said as much as he introduced his meagre story.

"When I remember Christmas," said Ndingi, "what comes to mind is a humble home, a wheeled contraption, a noisy episode and words etched on the lips of a lonely old man. But these cluttered relics of a worn memory have all these years (I am forty two now) constituted for me a riddle. A riddle which—like life, that larger puzzle most of us carry, yet wade through to the grave and never unravel the purpose of our being. It has been the truth that some of our most profound and lingering experiences come not heralded, but flow hence as taints in the clear waters of innocence, clouding it to oblivion in their very tint.

"I suppose this hardly makes for new insight, but you ask that tender age of innocence to relive for you its wonder? Its demise? Oh, I wouldn't know how to— I hardly fit the task!"

Ndingi then looked at his attentive audience and, with a somewhat defeated smile playing on his lips, said, "Seeing that I am out numbered here, it is best if I told the story as suggested. I'll settle scores with the host at a more opportune time." This elicited a number of chuckles that quickly died down in anticipation of Ndingi's story.

A moment later, a thrill of excitement ran through him as he agonized in the perennial thespian anxiety over whether he would succeed in capturing his subject. But leaving that for his audience to decide he began to reminisce about his "clattered relics of a worn memory."

"My name is Ndingi Kimuna. I am six-years-old. Christmas—that morning I was playing marbles by myself outside our house. Where we live—okay—it's not a house like, y'know, on its own compound and stuff, it is a rented room among many others. It is made of wooden walls, unpainted. The roof is of corrugated iron sheets, black on the inside because of smoke which mother says has accumulated over the years.

"The house would be ugly but for the floor. It is made of concrete. And it was polished with a red stain when the houses were being built. When mother washes it in the morning before going to her stall at the market, it shines and makes the house kind of look beautiful. That's why I like our house. I always wonder, though, for in the evening, no matter how dirty it may be, the dirt doesn't show when the lamp is on. Mother says it's my imagination but I don't believe her.

"Our row of houses face the road but nobody can see us from the other side because of a eucalyptus fence. This is where I was playing, on our side of the fence, while wondering what secret Mother was cooking inside (she wouldn't tell me but I could smell a part of it—*chapatis*) when I heard a familiar sound up the road. A sound like – y'know, like - like small empty cans rattling in confined space? That kind of noise. It was being made by an old—yes! a vintage—I'd heard somebody call it a vintage Ford Anglia. It belongs to our landlord.

"I stopped in my playing and watched it enter the compound on its wobbly wheels, trailing thick black smoke before it choked and coughed to a halt.

"The Landlord—he looked drunk, and before I could say hello he banged shut the car door and staggered to Kiarie's house, the first on our row. The door opened even before he could knock and there stood Kiarie facing him between the door frames. He is sixty-years-old and a widower, he told me that himself.

"'Merry Christmas, Mr Ngotho,' he greeted the landlord and smiled.

"'I s'ppose you have the money today, Kiarie?' enquired the landlord without answering to the greetings. 'You are one month in arrears, remember?'

"'Yes, I remember, Mr. Ngotho, but I - '

"'Don't have the money,' the landlord finished the sentence for him. 'Is that it? And you dare Merry Christmas me?'

"'Mr Ngotho, I —'

"'You listen to me!' the landlord shouted cutting him short. 'I am not made of money, you hear?! And my rooms are not for charity!'

"'Please, Mr — ' Kiarie tried to say something but the Landlord continued.

"It's people like you who make us miserable
—"

"'Please don't be—'

"'You listen to me!' the landlord shouted even
louder, then in Kiswahili abusively called him,
'taka taka wewe!' and spat on the ground.

"'There's no need to be upset, Mr Ngotho,'
Kiarie finally managed to say as the landlord glared
at him panting with anger. 'I do -'

"'Do? Huh?!' the landlord yelled, 'I'll tell you
what you are going to do: You have five days—
until New Year! You hear! New Year! Then you
are going to sleep outside like a lorry!

"Then, surprising even the landlord, Kiarie
thrust his hand to give something. It had been
there all along, the thick roll of money, which the
landlord snatched and stomped unsteadily to his
car that had trouble starting, before rattling off in
a cloud of smoke.

"I was surprised that Kiarie did not look angry,
but as the clearing smoke swirled about him,
making him look like he was on fire, he muttered
to himself, 'People! who understands people!'"

Ndingi paused, signalling that he had finished
his narrative. But whether he had succeeded in
telling it like a six-year-old could not have left

many doubts. The appreciative round of hand claps told it all.

Assuming his normal self again, Ndingi concluded his story. "Kiarie moved from our plot the following month. I know that he went back to his native Kinangop where he lived to be eighty. But about my riddle, I don't pretend any poetic abilities, but this is it: 'People, who are they? Are they a home or a wheeled contraption, a noisy episode or a few words on lips of a lonely old man? People, who are they?'

"I never could answer that question, and I never have, and perhaps that is why I became an actor to discover people's essences by being them. But it always seems to me I grew up on that Christmas day, when I was six years old."

MARY

MARY KATHAMBI was too unwell to do anything. The disturbing question on her mind as she sat on a low stool outside her mother's house was, 'Do I tell them now that I have it?'

She was referring to her two young sons, Mwiti, who was five, and Kimathi, who was three. These two boys were playfully chasing each other near the cow-shed not too far from where Mary sat.

It was about ten o'clock in the morning and the sun shone on the hilly Nyambene landscape. This Mary was overseeing from the high ridge that was her home making her think that the land looked like a beautiful picture of various shades of green. This she especially noted because, though the sun shone with vitality bringing out all the beauty of the land, she felt too sick to enjoy it. But as she listened to her children calling to each other and laughing heartily in their game, the pain she felt was not just physical. It was an intense feeling of guilt that terribly wrenched her heart for what it would mean for the children after she was gone.

What would become of them she would not dare to imagine, the irony being that it was them in their innocence who stood to suffer the hardest blows. The pain she felt because of this defied words.

But the question on her mind persisted, and she kept asking herself, 'but how does a mother tell her young children that she has full blown AIDS that is killing her little by little day by day?'

Indeed, this question had been with her for many days, for the children must be eventually told. And Mary wanted to be the one to tell them and not her widowed mother whom she lived with, and who took care of the three of them.

'Still, how must they be told? Would they understand?' Mary wondered. All the two boys knew was that their "Mami" had been sick for a long time, and she had grown a little thin and was unable to do anything, though she still kept her reassuring motherly smile.

Mary looked towards her children with a heavy heart and it passed through her mind how it all began in Meru town where she once lived and worked as a secretary.

She was not sure when but she must have contracted the disease after Mwiti, her first son, was born. Before then she had a steady lover, Kamenchu, who had fled when he heard she was pregnant. It was after Mwiti was born that she started having affairs with a few other men. This had inevitably led to her second pregnancy. And it was towards the end of this pregnancy that her world had disintegrated. A blood test had revealed that she was HIV positive.

This revelation had been devastating. And not knowing where to turn to, Mary had nearly committed suicide. But knowing that she had to talk to someone, she had gone to her mother who was adversely affected by the news, for Mary was the last born and the favourite of five children. However, Mary's mother, and her family in general, had taken the tragedy with compassion and accorded the pregnant Mary the love and understanding she needed. It was in this loving atmosphere that Kimathi, her second son was born.

He too had been diagnosed as HIV positive at birth. But 'by the grace of God,' as everyone who knew gratefully put it, Kimathi's diagnosis had gradually turned negative as he grew up. Now three years old and running around, he was as healthy and as HIV free as his brother, Mwiti. Mary felt it had been some kind of miracle.

And then, without warning, a bout of pneumonia had suddenly got her. And after she had recovered from it, a multitude of other illness had come one after another so that she could no longer work. AIDS had set in. Since then she and her children had been living with her mother.

Mary blew her nose and wet her dry lips, and did not care to remember any more of the history of her troubles. It was too painful. Instead she thought of her mother who, as if on cue, stepped from the house and came directly to where she sat, almost as if she knew her daughter needed some comforting.

As she reached Mary, the mother observed, "What a fine morning," but noticing her daughter's pained expression, she quickly said, "You don't feel well..." Which was more of a statement than a question. But before she could finish what she was saying, Mary interrupted and said, "I must tell the children now, mother. But what must I tell them?"

Mary's mother did not bother to ask her daughter why it should be now, but after a moment she replied, "The Truth, Mary. Tell them the truth."

"Maami has something she wants to say to you," said the grandmother to the children after calling them to her. "But please don't cry, everything will be alright," she added.

Then Mary said with great difficulty, "You know I have been sick for a long time..." then she cleared her throat and paused briefly as if unsure of what to say. "Well," she continued haltingly, "I...I am dying of a disease called AIDS." She wanted to but she could say no more as she choked with emotion.

Mwiti first looked at his mother then at his grandmother with disbelief. Then he heard his brother Kimathi ask their mother, "What is dying, maami?"

Mary could say nothing but cry.

That night she fell into a coma and never woke up.

RUMOURS

AH, BUT—RUMOURS! Tch! They are a curious phenomenon. How or where they start I'll never understand. And once they start, they respect neither time or distance, for within no time you will hear them afire in people's hearts in places as remote and as distant as the hills and the plains. But that is not all. They also seem to have a peculiar tendency to transform themselves by the hour. What you hear today is not what you hear tomorrow. It is as if it is themselves and not the mouths that twist this product of their tongues so ingeniously.

Take, for instance, what happened to Muraya not so long ago. The rumuor that was to haunt him for many days started in just such a manner— seemingly out of nowhere. To those who don't know him, he can easily be marked out from a distance. He walks with hunched shoulders, like one carrying a heavy load; spots a tired, shuffling gait that foretells his quiet and extremely timid disposition. A condition that has condemned him to bachelorhood, even though he is nudging forty now.

But to understand what triggered the rumour, let me first explain the incident that preceded it.

Now, Old Man Kang'ethe needs no introduction to you, and as you well know, his land borders that of Muraya. It so happens that this border between them has a long and troubled history of disputes. But when they started nobody knows. They are said to have started during the time of their fathers' fathers—way back when. The issue stands unresolved to day for lack of reliable facts which seem to have changed with each successful generation and therefore, as it were, amount to no more than hearsay. Even the council of elders long washed its hands off the dispute.

Anyway, Old Man Kang'ethe had revived this difficult matter. He wanted to settle the dispute "once and for all," and with this in mind had accosted Muraya about it. But Muraya, despite his timidity which the old man supposedly was taking advantage of, revealed a streak of stubbornness previously unknown to have existed in him. He said he knew nothing about the border. All he knew, he said to the face of Old Man Kang'ethe, was that the land including its borders was left to him by his father (he was an only son), and was not going to budge an inch of it. "And that is that", Muraya had finished with surprising firmness.

Now, while Old Man Kang'ethe had expected that they would at least talk it over, he had deemed Muraya as being unnecessarily impudent and had taken this response unkindly.

This seemed so because, intended or not, it amounted to saying that Kang'ethe knew not what he was talking about, which was a terrible insult to his age. But he is a temperamental old man, as everybody knows, and true to his fiery temper he had sprung like a wounded animal and in his anger had repeatedly struck Muraya with his spiked walking stick, drawing blood.

The unsurprising thing was that despite the pain and the public humiliation, Muraya had not struck back and said nothing even as he ran away from his enraged assailant.

The matter seemed to have ended there, but one cold morning, Old Man Kang'ethe's cow, Ngamo, named so for it's enormous and fruitful udder, failed to produce milk. By midday, a rumour had started making the rounds: that Muraya, on account of his public humiliation by the old man, had bewitched the cow.

We might as well leave Old Man Kang'ethe out of it for who started the rumour, or where, your guess is as good as mine. But from then on, the man whom everybody knew to be as harmless and as humble as a lamb suddenly acquired the reputation of an evil and deadly wizard. Indeed, some people started saying they had suspected he was that all along.

Then another rumour started that he, in fact, had been sighted approaching Old Man Kang'ethe's homestead the night before the cow cut its milk. It further went on to say that Muraya was in a wizard's full gear and eerie paraphernalia, complete with a smoking human skull. Never mind that in the history of our people, as far as I can recall there never has been the likes of such a wizard. Witchdoctors or medicinemen, yes, but wizards? You can trust the people's fertile imagination for that.

By the following day, as the rumour intensified, it had completely changed, somewhat. It now purported that Muraya had actually been sighted running naked around a tree near his adversary's homestead chanting incorrigible but ominous sounding words in its direction. It further purported that he had been heard swearing that he would not stop until he had finished Old Man Kang'ethe, who took it all calmly and went about his life oblivious of the rumours.

But some people started following Muraya to see what he would do, and when night came kept a vigil near his home. Nothing came of their trouble but the rumour persisted that he had been seen somewhere or other in this or that unsavoury act.

They never seemed to run out of ideas. Even Muraya's ancestors were not spared. The rumours had it that they too were responsible for the assortment of ills, real or imagined, that had plagued the village. The full extent of this was that even Muraya's relatives disowned him in order to save the sanctity of their insulted ancestors.

Days came and went and the rumours did not stop, despite the fact that Ngamo, the cow, had resumed its plentiful supply of milk. But Muraya bore it admirably, inspite of being shunned and spat on.

Days passed. Then the strain of being a pariah began to tell on him. He began to lose weight and started falling prey to opportunistic illnesses. Unable to take it any more, a gaunt and sickly looking Muraya, who in those short days had even grown grey hair, finally went to Chief Wamunyu.

After explaining his troubles to the chief, who listened sympathetically and said little until this victim of public paranoia had finished, Chief Wamunyu, who is a master in the subtleties of simple analogy, calmly asked him, "What would you do to snuff out a raging bush fire?"

Muraya, despite his obvious surprise at the question, didn't hesitate and answered promptly, "Having no otherwise you let it burn itself out, sir."

"Precisely," responded the chief. "So it is with

118

rumours. Just be yourself and be strong. They will come to pass."

Muraya departed feeling a little better and the matter might have ended there for him. Indeed, the rumours would soon come to an end. Yet within that hour of leaving the chief, another rumour had started: That Muraya had finally recanted his evil ways.

The details in the rumour were elaborate. They purported that unable to contain his evil spirits, which had been harassed by people's discontent, Muraya had voluntarily taken all his wares, which included a black chicken, a human skull— ah! It is senseless to name them—the paraphernalia which the rumour said he took to the chief, at whose feet he dumped them and started a mysterious bush-fire and ...!

Tch! rumours! See how they twist the truth!